TEDD

Book 5

The Rev Patrick Ashe is a retired vicar
who has worked for many years for the
cause of children, having been a chap-
lain for youth and the founder of two
relief organisations: Project Vietnam
Orphans and Christian Outreach. He
has seven children who were the first
to hear these stories before they were
written down for a wider audience.

By the same author:
Teddy Brown Finds a Home
Teddy Brown is Rescued
Teddy Brown's Secret
Teddy Brown and the Battle

Teddy Brown Goes on Holiday

Pat Ashe

KINGSWAY PUBLICATIONS
EASTBOURNE

Text illustrations and cover design by John Dillow

British Library Cataloguing in Publication Data

Ashe, Pat
 Teddy Brown goes on holiday.
 I. Title   II. Series
 823'.914 [J]

 ISBN 0-86065-782-5

Printed in Great Britain for
KINGSWAY PUBLICATIONS LTD
1 St Anne's Road, Eastbourne, E Sussex BN21 3UN by
Stanley L. Hunt (Printers) Ltd, Rushden, Northants.
Typeset by Nuprint Ltd, Harpenden, Herts AL5 4SE.

For Robert
and all the children who listen
to these stories

Contents

A WORD TO
PARENTS AND TEACHERS

You may find the stories in this fifth book about
Teddy Brown helpful as 'starters' in getting children to think about Christian behaviour. Toy
Soldier learns about humility; Teddy Brown dis-
covers some of the ways God answers prayer, and
he helps Bulldog find out that Jesus was more
than a good man.

At the end of the book there are suggested Bible
readings if you should want to get children used to
handling a Bible. I recommend using a modern
translation such as J. B. Phillips or *The Living
Bible*.

1

TOY SOLDIER GOES TO THE ROYAL GARDEN PARTY

One day Toy Soldier got a letter. Everybody had a look at it before he opened it because it had the Royal Crest on the back.

When Toy Soldier opened it he nearly fell out of the Toy Cupboard. It was from the Queen, inviting him to a Royal Garden Party at Buckingham Palace. It said that she was inviting certain members of her Armed Forces, and trusted he would attend.

There was great excitement, and everyone said they would come and watch him go into the Palace.

Toy Soldier had not been wearing his uniform much lately. His wife said it was because he had put on a bit of weight. But Toy Soldier said it was because he was more comfortable in his flannel trousers and sports jacket.

When his wife got his uniform out, he said, 'I'm not going to wear that. I'm going in my flannels and sports jacket.'

Teddy Brown tried to persuade him to wear the Queen's uniform, but he said, 'You mind your own business!'

Once Toy Soldier had made up his mind, nothing would change him. So his wife did her best. She pressed his trousers, and sponged his jacket, and off he went.

The other toys went with him and stood by the railings of Buckingham Palace.

Toy Soldier went up to the gate. The sentry stepped forwards. 'Hey!' he said. 'Where d'you think you're going?'

'I'm going to the Garden Party.'

'It's for Her Majesty's Forces only,' said the sentry.

'I'm a sergeant,' said Toy Soldier.

'I don't care who you are, you're not coming in like that.'

Toy Soldier was furious—his moustache began to bristle, and he tried to push past the sentry. But the sentry called the guard, and they threw Toy Soldier out. He stood outside the railings, shouting and swearing and shaking his fist.

When they were home again, Teddy Brown took Toy Soldier off on his own. He said, 'I

remember a story I once heard in church. It was about a king whose son was going to be married.'

'Well, what about it?' grunted Toy Soldier.

'All the people he had invited wouldn't go, so he sent out an invitation to the poor people and the beggars, and to those who had no homes and were hungry.'

'They must have been a funny looking lot at the prince's wedding—all dressed in dirty old clothes.'

'That's what they said. They said, "But we can't go in like this—we'd be ashamed." But the messenger said, "Don't worry, the King is going to provide you with a wedding robe to put on."'

'So as each guest arrived, the King's Chamberlain said, "Will you step this way, and put on the King's gift?" It was a beautiful white robe, a wedding garment. They put it on and sat down.'

Teddy Brown began to get cold feet about the story—he was afraid Toy Soldier would see why he was telling it, and bash him. But he screwed up courage and went on. 'One man didn't accept the King's gift. "Oh, no thanks," he said. "I'll be all right as I am." He was in a pair of grey flannel trousers and a sports jacket.'

Toy Soldier's moustache began to bristle—he was very angry. But then he said, 'All right—go on. I'll listen.'

Teddy Brown went on, 'The man sat down

12

with all the others, but he felt very uncomfortable. They were all in white, and he felt dirty.'

Toy Soldier began to think about the Garden Party. He wondered what he would have felt like if he had gone in without his uniform. He wondered what the Queen would have said. Toy Soldier began to pull at his moustache, and it drooped.

Then Teddy Brown went on, 'When the King came in, he looked round and saw the man who was not wearing his gift. The King said, "Friend, how did you come in here without the wedding garment?" The man did not know what to say.'

Toy Soldier was glad no one else was listening to Teddy Brown's story, because there was worse to come. Teddy Brown went on, 'The King said, "Take that man and throw him out into the dark, where he will weep and grind his teeth." '

Toy Soldier thought about what he had done outside the railings at Buckingham Palace. He felt terrible. It was then that he noticed that Robby had come in. He tried to look tough again. He bristled up his moustache, and said, 'Teddy Brown has been telling me a story that he says is in the Bible, but I don't believe it.'

'Well, it is,' said Robby. 'It is one of the stories Jesus told, and it means that God won't let us into heaven unless we put on the wedding robe he has provided.'

'What robe has he provided?' asked Toy Soldier.

Teddy Brown answered, because he knew.

'Jesus,' he said. 'Jesus wraps us up in the Holy Spirit so that we can get to God.'

'What about the man who did not accept the King's gift?'

'He was the one who thought he was good enough to get to God without the Holy Spirit— without the King's gift, and you know what happened to him!'

Toy Soldier was very quiet. Then he went off and sat in a corner of the Toy Cupboard for a few days, and said he had a headache.

2

THE VOICE

The whole family had been down at the seaside, and on the way home they were invited to stay overnight with some friends in Brockenhurst in the New Forest.

Although the toys had been in a train before, they had always been packed up in a suitcase. But this time Teddy Brown and Pink Rabbit were near the top of Robby's bag. They were so anxious to look out of the train window that they climbed out of the bag and stood watching the trees and houses flashing by.

'I wonder where they are all going to,' said Pink Rabbit.

Teddy Brown said, 'They're not going anywhere; it's us who are going. The houses are all standing still.'

Pink Rabbit tried to think that out, but it sent her brain into a whirl, so she shut her eyes and went to sleep. After a while Teddy Brown went to sleep as well.

When they got to Brockenhurst the whole family got off the train, and did not notice Teddy Brown and Pink Rabbit asleep in a corner. But when they got to their friends' house and began unpacking, Robby could not find Teddy Brown and Pink Rabbit.

'Has anyone seen Teddy Brown?' he asked.

But no one had.

Robby went into his room to pray: 'Dear Lord Jesus, Teddy Brown and Pink Rabbit have got lost. Please look after them and bring them safely back.'

Then he thought, 'I'll go to the station and see if they are there. If they stayed on the train, they might come back.'

So he went and waited on the platform at Brockenhurst, and as each train came in from London, he looked for them.

When Teddy Brown woke up he gave Pink Rabbit a nudge. 'Pink Rabbit—they've all gone!'

They called and called, and looked along the corridor, but there was no sign of Robby or the family.

Pink Rabbit began to cry. 'Oh dear! We should never have climbed out of Robby's bag, then we would have got out with all the others. And now we'll never find them.' And she wailed, 'Oh, Oh, we'll never see them again.'

Teddy Brown wanted to cry too, but he took long breaths so that he could comfort Pink Rabbit.

The train rushed on and stopped a few times, but they did not know what to do, so they sat still. Finally it stopped for a longer time, and everyone got out. A man shouted, 'Waterloo—all change, all change, all change!' so they got out too.

Then Teddy Brown remembered that Robby had said they were going to get out at Brockenhurst. He said to Pink Rabbit, 'We must find a train going to Brockenhurst. I'm sure Robby will be looking for us.'

There were hundreds of people all hurrying in different directions. Teddy Brown saw a man sitting on his luggage. 'Please Sir,' he said. 'Can you tell me which train goes to Brockenhurst?'

'Yes,' the man replied. 'I think it's the one that leaves from platform three.'

So they hurried to platform three. There was a nice man at the barrier.

'Does this train go to Brockenhurst?'

'No, it's the one at platform thirteen,' he replied, 'but you'll have to hurry.'

They ran as fast as they could, and got to

platform thirteen just in time to see the back of a train leaving the station.

Tears began to dribble down Pink Rabbit's nose. 'We'll never see them again,' she said.

But Teddy Brown was not going to give up. He saw a kind looking lady and went up to her. Very politely he said, 'Excuse me, Madam, but do you know which platform the next train to Brockenhurst leaves from?'

'Ah,' she said, 'let me see. Brockenhurst—yes. That will probably be on the Portsmouth line. Try platform seven.'

They went to platform seven, but Brockenhurst was not on that line at all.

Even Teddy Brown was beginning to get frightened. Suddenly he said, 'Pink Rabbit—we haven't prayed! Let's ask Jesus.'

They went into a quiet corner and shut their eyes. 'Please God,' they prayed, 'help us to get back to Brockenhurst.'

And then they heard a VOICE. It was a big booming voice that filled the whole station. It said, 'The next train to Bournemouth will leave from platform eleven, stopping at Woking, Basingstoke, Brockenhurst and Southampton.'

When she heard 'Brockenhurst', Pink Rabbit gave a squeal of joy. 'Teddy Brown, God has answered our prayer. That was his voice. He said it was going to stop at Brockenhurst.'

18

Before they rushed off to platform eleven, they shut their eyes again: 'Thank you, dear Lord, for telling us where to go.'

When they got into the train, they made sure they did not go to sleep, and they spelled out the name of each station when the train stopped there. They nearly got out at Basingstoke because it was a long word beginning with a 'B'.

But finally it said 'Brockenhurst', and they got out. And there was Robby waiting on the platform. He gave them both a hug, and said, 'I knew you would find your way back.'

On the way to their friends' house, Pink Rabbit said, 'Robby, God's got a very loud voice. When he told us which train to catch, everybody in the station must have heard it.'

Teddy Brown said, 'Robby, was it really God's voice?'

Robby thought a bit, and then he said, 'Yes, it was God speaking and answering your prayer, but the voice actually came from a man in an office talking through loudspeakers.'

'Does God always speak through loudspeakers?' asked Pink Rabbit.

'No, not always. Sometimes he speaks through a friend who gives us right advice, or he speaks through a sermon in church. But very often he speaks through the Bible. As we read it, we know what he wants us to do.'

20

Teddy Brown rubbed his nose and scratched his ear. Then he said, 'Robby, you once told me to be quiet and listen when I pray. That's when we heard the voice. Sometimes when I'm praying, and get quiet, a little thought comes into my mind. Is that God speaking?'

'Yes,' said Robby, 'if it is the sort of thing Jesus would say, telling you to do something that Jesus would do.'

When they got to the house, the other toys said, 'Well, we never thought we would ever see either of you again.'

Pink Rabbit said, 'Do you know how we got back? God spoke to us through a loudspeaker.'

Toy Soldier gave a snort, and said, 'Silly cuckoo.'

But some of the other toys wanted to know more, and Teddy Brown told them what Robby had said.

BULLDOG TRIES TO BE GOOD

Mr Woollyhead was a doll who thought that everybody could be good if they really wanted to and if they tried hard enough. He was always giving the others good advice. He would say things like 'Keep smiling', and 'Don't worry'. His motto was 'Never do anybody any harm', and he wanted everyone to be kind and friendly. He was a very nice doll.

Now, near them lived a great big bulldog. He had a large chest, a big heavy head with a flat nose and two long side teeth. He had a bark that made everyone jump, and a growl that made most people run for a tree. He used to swagger down the road, and if he did not like the look of a person's face, he would go for them. It's a horrid thing to say, but he was just a great big swaggering bully.

Mr Woollyhead thought this was dreadful—and, of course, it was.

One day, when Bulldog was resting after an excellent meal, Mr Woollyhead thought it might be a good chance to have a talk with him. He said, 'Mr Bulldog, I hope you won't mind me telling you this, but you know, everyone is beginning to dislike you. You are soon going to be the most hated dog in town.'

Bulldog opened his mouth to take a bite out of Mr Woollyhead's pants, but then he realised that Mr Woollyhead was really trying to be helpful, so he decided to listen. He said, 'Well, what do you think I ought to do?'

Mr Woollyhead took a deep breath, and began, 'You must be a good dog, kind and gentle. You must love everybody and not chase cats. When somebody bites your ear, you must let them bite the other one.'

Bulldog looked to see whether he was trying to pull his leg. 'Where did you get those ideas from?' he said.

'There is a book,' replied Mr Woollyhead, 'about a man called Jesus. He was a great teacher, and told us how we ought to live.'

Bulldog said, 'Do you do what he said?'

Mr Woollyhead looked a bit uneasy. 'Well, I try,' he said. 'Why don't you try?'

To his amazement, Bulldog said,

'All right, I'm willing to try anything once. Let's start.'

So they looked up some of the things that Jesus had told his followers to do. Mr Woollyhead read out: 'If some one takes your coat, give him your cloak as well.'

'That's OK,' said Bulldog. 'My coat won't come off so no one can pinch it, and I haven't got a cloak.'

Mr Woollyhead went on, 'Love your enemies, and do good to those who treat you spitefully.'

Not many people treated Bulldog spitefully, so he nodded.

But when Mr Woollyhead read, 'When someone asks you for something, give it to him; when someone wants to borrow something, lend it to him,' Bulldog interrupted. 'But that's too much,' he said. 'It's impossible. I don't think anyone could do what Jesus says. I'm sure I can't.'

But Bulldogs have great determination. So as he had said he would try, try he did! He tried not to growl, and he tried not to mind when the cats called him a cissy. He tried not to take other dogs' bones—but when other dogs took away his bones, it took all the will power he had not to tear them to pieces.

Now, Bulldog had one great friend, a sheep dog, and they were real buddies. He was fond of Sheepdog, and used to spend a lot of time with him because it was easy to do what the man Jesus said when he was with Sheepdog.

But one day Bulldog had buried a really nice juicy bone. He had been very careful not to let anyone see where he had hidden it, but the next day when he went to get it, he found Sheepdog had dug it up and was eating it. Bulldog just saw red, and by the time he was finished with him, poor Sheepdog was torn and bleeding.

Mr Woollyhead went to Bulldog. 'That was very wrong of you,' he said. 'You must go and say you're sorry.'

'Never,' growed Bulldog, and he looked so fierce that Mr Woollyhead thought he had better see what the view looked like from the top of the nearest tree.

Then Bulldog began to feel very ashamed. He went off and hid, and the more he thought, the worse he felt. He had broken all his good resolutions, but he would never say sorry.

While he was thinking, Teddy Brown came up. He always told the truth to Teddy Brown.

'Oh, Teddy Brown,' he said. 'I've done a dreadful thing—I've bitten and torn my best friend, all over a silly bone. I've tried to be a Christian and do all the things Jesus said, but I can't. I'm always failing, though I've been pretending to old Woollyhead that I'm doing all right. But I can't. I'm just a miserable, weak-willed, bad-tempered flop.

I'm going to give it all up, and go back to my old ways.'

Teddy Brown rubbed his nose and scratched his ear. Then he said, 'Would you like to know where you have gone wrong, Bulldog?'

'Yes.'

'The reason you have not succeeded is because you have only half the truth.'

'Oh, what's the other half then?'

'The other half of the truth is that Jesus is alive now, and that his Spirit can come into you and make you able to do what he says.'

'But how can he still be alive? Mr Woollyhead says he died two thousand years ago.'

'Yes, he did, but he rose again from the dead, and he is still alive now.'

Bulldog looked amazed. 'But no one has ever done that—risen from the dead, and stayed alive for two thousand years!'

'You see, Bulldog,' said Teddy Brown, 'Jesus was not just a man, he was God. It is his Spirit that is still alive and can be with us and in us. He not only gave us rules for life, but promised to give us his strength so that we can carry them out.'

There was a long pause. Then Bulldog said, 'Of course, I see now. I've been trying to do it all by will power.'

'And now what you need is for Jesus to give you his Spirit.'

Then Teddy Brown told him how Jesus had changed his life, and about a verse that Robby had taught him, something St Paul said, 'That Christ may dwell in your hearts by faith.'

'I'd like Jesus to live in my heart,' said Bulldog.

Teddy Brown and Bulldog went across the road into church and up to the altar rail, and if you had looked in you would have seen Teddy Brown kneeling, and Bulldog with his paws up on the rail.

Bulldog told Jesus he was sorry for all the bad things he had done, and asked Jesus to forgive him. Then he asked him to come into his heart and give him a new spirit.

When they went out, Bulldog felt different. He went straight to Sheepdog and said he was sorry. He found that it was not just that he *ought* to love everybody—with Jesus he really *did* love them. He wanted everyone to know what Jesus had done for him. Then he went to Mr Woollyhead and said, 'You only told me half the truth. You told me what Jesus said, but you never told me he was alive and could make me want to do those things, and give me strength to do them.'

Mr Woollyhead did not know what to say, because he had never discovered that Jesus could come and live in his heart. But when he saw the

real change in Bulldog, he began to think that perhaps Teddy Brown was right, and that Jesus really was still alive.

Suggested Bible Readings

1. Toy Soldier Goes to the Royal Garden Party

Matthew 22:8–14.

2. The Voice

1 Kings 19:11–13.
Isaiah 30:21.

3. Bulldog Tries to Be Good

Matthew 5:38–44; 16:15–16.
Ephesians 3:16–19.